Contemporary Stories of Otherness

Joanna Łukasiewicz

Viktoria Kos

Andrii Kurbyko

Sarah Wilhelm

Edited by

Bulent Akman & Emma Oki

ISBN-13: 9798481607214

DEDICATION

Great students make great teachers and vice versa.

"It is not your responsibility to finish the work of perfecting the world, but you are not free to desist from it either."
Rabbi Tarfon, Pirkei Avoth 2:21

CONTENTS

ACKNOWLEDGMENTS

Our sincere thanks to Dr. Emma Oki.
whose initiative and vision made this book possible.

WOLF'S PATH
BY
JOANNA ŁUKASIEWICZ

A year ago, he was banished from the city. From that moment, Wolf was on the run from the furious magnates.

But exile was not enough. Full of revenge, they followed his trail.

He managed to lose them only by swimming across the Great River.

Since childhood, he feared water.

The vivid ache of the cold river slicing into his body made his knees tremble and his heart beat faster.

'It's okay, you are safe.' Wolf said. The words didn't comfort him so he lay back down in his small boat, cuddling Milo's soft fur.

The boat was drifting downstream. Wolf let the river set their pace. He didn't have the soul of the marauder, but fate constantly drove him to stalemates in which the only way out was to break the law.

'Maybe the world is constructed this way. We are not born bad, we only become so.' Milo answered with an impassive voice. 'It's good to have you, buddy. You are the only one who doesn't judge me.

Wolf raised his head to see where the water carried them. The sun was setting and a wind blowing from the north promised a cool night. It was time to find a place to light a fire and warm tired bones. He grabbed the oars and rowed to the nearest shore. Wolf could feel ghosts and mares coming in the air, waiting for loners like him. In the light of day, they were not so threatening and confident, but they lurked in the dark to deceive their victims. The weaker fell to paranoia, which continued even after the night had passed. Poor men became lunatics and an object of ridicule in their towns and villages.

Luckily, Milo with his astonishing sense of smell was able to detect dark powers from a great distance. Wolf himself knew some protection spells that he had learned from a tree shaman. All he needed was a fire.

Milo quickly jumped from the boat, wagging his tail cheerfully. Wolf didn't have time to call after him when the dog disappeared into the thicket of the forest chasing the rabbit, sniffing at every bush. Wolf, accustomed to this, ostentatiously exhaled and began to pull the boat to the river bank. Although he was sure that in this area there was no one around to rob him, he still tied his old boat securely to a tree if only to avoid it drifting away. Then he looked for a place to light a small fire. He had less than an hour to make it before dark. He walked towards the forest, carefully looking around while summoning his dog.

Time was running out and he was still running breakneck through the woods.

***

Milo sank into the ground. He was lost. he couldn't find the rabbit, he couldn't find the river either. The temperature was constantly dropping as if the ghosts were preparing for a feast. His calm disappeared, making room for a creeping feeling of danger.

***

'Where is that damn dog?' Wolf said bitterly. In moments like this, Milo's presence buoyed him up.

Although the sun has not yet fully set, he strained his senses. He wanted to hear any signs of impending danger; it could be the slightest rustle.

'Bloody hell, if it goes on like this, I'll end up a vegetable.' He speeded up. He ran into the forest in the direction he'd last seen Milo, brushing away visibility-limiting branches. His movements became nervous, which made maneuvering harder. The canopy overhead thickened, allowing less of already-failing light to reach the ground. Wolf felt like he was losing track of time and was unable to tell which way he was going. He paused to catch his breath and realized he'd lost his conditioning. He couldn't run a mile anymore without panting.

The moment passed, his heart slowed its pounding. Resigned, he sat on a log lying across the forest moss and began to listen to the singing birds. However, he had a feeling that amongst the twitter he was hearing another sound, similar to human speech.

'Am I having hallucinations?' he didn't get the answer.

Wolf was not sure if the ghosts were already playing with him or maybe in the remote wilderness, he came across a trace of human life. As quiet as possible he began to follow the woman's voice. He feared the worst. It could be a trap. After all, the forest was already dim and ghosts could sense the presence of a man for many miles. Without a bonfire and protecting spells, he was an easy target for ravenous souls.

The voice became clearer, you could even say - mellifluous. Something so pleasant for the ear couldn't have wrong intentions. He took every step carefully, not wanting to attract any attention. He crouched behind the bush to cover his body, while being able to observe the woman from a safe distance.

A few dozen feet away began small glade surrounded by trees planted at an equal distance. In the center of a glade there was a woman dressed in an earthy, coquettishly tight dress. Black, waist-length hair lightly fluttered in the wind as she was walking around the small bonfire, continuing to utter protective spells.

Elements of the day,
Elements of the sun,
Come this way.
Powers of night and day,
I summon thee,
I call upon thee,
To protect me.

The words blended, even though Wolf knew their content perfectly. Whispers were echoing the woman's words from all sides. Her image became cloudy as if he was looking at her from beneath the water's surface. He was in the daze and the visions kept coming into his head. He clung to the branch sticking out of the ground because he was afraid that he would lose the earth under his feet.

'You must not peek at people, traveler.' the woman materialized next to him and grabbed his arm with her slim hand.

Wolf stood up and shook the leaves off. He had to blink a few times to make sure the person standing in front of him was not a phantom.

'Please forgive me, but I wasn't sure if I could disturb you.

'Call me Meredith. What brings you here, traveler?'

'I'm an outcast seeking shelter. I stopped at this area to look for a glade, and just like you, light the campfire. I thought I wouldn't make it before the night when I heard your voice.'

'You have chosen a risky path, traveler. Don't you hear about ghosts living in the wood?'

The woman moved toward the glade without looking at him.

'Well, I didn't have a choice.' Wolf followed her. 'And you? I dare say that a place like this is not the safest place for a woman.'

'I am an Anchoress. The Lord of the Light takes care of my body and soul.'

The woman bent down to a long cane next to the fire and drew a circle around the burning branches, whispering under her breath. She seemed to be floating in the air. Wolf was watching the anchoresses' every move carefully because he has never met one before. However, he has heard a lot of gossip about their bizarre behaviors. Kidnapping children, eating reptiles, draining and consuming animal blood. It was also said that they were relying on dark magic. The fact of living in places far away from people was also not helpful in saving their reputation.

Unlike local priestesses, who lived in temples and prayed during each great feast together with the faithful, Anchoresses did not enjoy widespread respect. Maybe because of that, they mastered the art of camouflage. Wolf had heard the superstition that an Anchoress could be found only if one had such a wish. He felt goosebumps all over his body, because he was still uncertain about her intentions. He was not sure what will be worse: one night with ghosts or with the Anchoress.

'Won't you be cold? In a thin outfit like yours, it's easy to catch a cold on a cool night.'

'Thank you for worrying.' a slight smile appeared on her face. She turned towards Wolf and looked at him profoundly. 'You don't behave like a typical outcast. I have to admit, it is a nice change. What's your name?'

'Wolf. It was my family's totem and I became their only descendant.'

'And you took that name to commemorate your ancestors?' the man nodded. 'Beautiful gesture.' Meredith invited him to sit next to her.'Wolf.' she repeated to herself. 'The symbol of combat, power, and independence. Your name will bring you a lot of challenges to face, traveler.'

Fog hung in the air and moans of tired souls searching for wandering unfortunates could be heard from afar. The smell of sulfur began to spread in the woods, changing its intensity from time to time. The singing of the birds has long ceased, even the trees have stopped whirring. The man felt relieved. A night away from campfire and magic in a completely haunted forest would be suicide. He wasn't aware how hard it would be to survive these conditions. Out of the blue he heard a loud whine.

'Milo!' Wolf sprang to his feet. He could recognize this sound everywhere.

'Have you lost your dog?' Meredith's face did not change expression, looking blankly at space.

The man did not answer, he was too busy listening for any signs of his friend's presence.

'I have to help him somehow.' he was walking around the edge of the glade, looking everywhere. Wolf didn't know what to do. If he went deep into the forest, the ghosts would certainly sense his presence, but he could not leave Milo there. He grew hesitant.

However, when he heard the whimper again he decided to act. He quickly ran to the other side of the glade. At the same moment, Red Wolf was about to wade through the brushwood, he bounced off some invisible matter which pushed him forcefully back.

'Are you a fool? Do you want to lose your mind today?' Meredith got up and looked at the man. 'For a dog? People just amaze me.'

'What have you done? What is it?' Wolf was trying to get to the other side, but he still met resistance. He felt like he was bouncing off a trampoline, like the ones he had seen in the circus. He was trying to get rid of the darkest thoughts from his head.

Wolf heard a snapping branch, Milo's howl was cut off by wet crunching like a pile of dry twigs torn in half.

'Milo...' tears started running down his cheeks as he crouched down at the edge of the woods. Red Wolf tried to control himself, but his body did not listen, constantly producing new drops. 'Sit by the fire, Wolf. Your crying won't help here.' Anchoress walked over the man, reaching out to him. The traveler pushed her away without taking his eyes off the trees. 'That is the law of this forest.' she continued, ignoring his condition. 'Tomorrow only one man can come out of it ... And it must be you.'

He frowned and looked at Meredith. The Anchoress lured him to this glade, as expected.

'If the Lord of the Light hadn't revealed to me your arrival in a vision, you would have lost your mind by now.' she pushed her hair back and continued. 'I decided that I would take a closer look at you and determine your chances of completing the task I want to entrust with you. Of course, you do not have to take it. If you refuse, I will let you go and you will forget about me and your dog the moment you leave this forest. You will continue your journey as an outlaw, wandering through forests, towns and villages, looking for some reason to live. But I suppose, sooner or later your influential enemies will hear about you and you will be forced to run away again.' Wolf said nothing, he was just listening to her words intermittently interrupted by the moan of wandering souls in the woods. Soul tears were rolling down his cheeks, which he occasionally wiped carelessly with his hand. For some time, he believed that his life had finally calmed down and that he would have a chance to live a peaceful life away from the people who banished him. He didn't know how wrong he was.

'I can give you life that no one can have. You can become everyone, but no one can become you. You will travel all around the world, meet new people, new places, but people won't know you. You will change your appearance when it will be needed. Imperceptible for your enemies, doesn't that sound good? As an unpunished man, you can escape from any consequences. And it will be your choice how you will use your new abilities.

'And what do you want in return?' he felt tired and sluggish. Wolf realized that he has not eaten since the morning. His stomach grumbled, which he tried to ignore.

'Find me a moonstone - a gem as ancient as the moon itself. Used properly it has powerful healing effects, that can even get rid of a deadly disease. If you find one, bring it to me. But do not try to fool me, because you will regret it bitterly. After your journey, I won't take your new skills from you, and you will be able to live your life without any threat from the enemies. Interested?

'Why can't you find it by yourself? You have so much power that you can give me skills I have never dreamed of, but you can't find some gem by yourself?' he outraged.

'How ironically. You people create absurd stories about us, that you feed generations. But you are never able to catch the truth about the inhabitants of the wilderness.' Meredith sighed. 'I am an Anchoress, that means I can't leave the place where I made my vows. Is it enough for you?'

Wolf nodded and Meredith turned on her heel.

'Give me your answer by morning.' she said without looking at him, then disappeared into the mist.

He was alone. Wolf sat down by the bonfire and began to think. Running away his whole life sounded like a plan, but he wasn't sure how long he could hide and sleep outside. Meredith proposed an alternative, that he could start all over again as a completely new man. He had lost his only friend and was wanted by the most influential man in the northern part of the country. What did he have to lose now?

***

Wolf woke up with sun rays falling on his face. He rubbed his eyes and looked around. Meredith was nowhere to be found, so how could he tell her his decision? Wolf moved ahead. He didn't know if he had already taken this route yesterday, but it didn't make any difference. He was listening to the sounds of nature and eating fresh berries while trying to erase the thought of his dog Milo from his memory. He was thinking about his next destination and which way was he was headed. The Anchoress didn't tell him where he could find a moonstone.

Wolf lost himself in his thoughts to such an extent, that he did not notice the end of the forest. He looked at the surface of the water glistening like a sheet of diamonds. A few seconds later he felt the energy flow into him. He decided, he would start searching for the gem in the capital of merchants, in the city called Oasis.

THE END

SWAN
BY
VIKTORIA KOŚCIEWICZ

Harry inched along the highway, his arm out the window, A lit cigarette between his fingers. Radio said the jam stretched all the way downtown.

A woman in the passenger seat stared at the cars and said 'I'm telling you the traffic here is always bad. That's why I told you to be at my place on time, baby.'

'You can be well-organised and all but don't patronize me. I know what I'm doing. We are not going to be late. Trust me for once. Goddammit.'

She looked at him.

'Did you bring my sweatshirt from your apartment? I asked you to, and stop smoking that damn cigarette. It stinks.'

'In traffic is when you decide to pick a fight?'

'Are we fighting? I only asked. Relax.'

They were on the bridge heading to the west side of the city. The traffic eased and Harry could speed up.

'Beth...'

She looked at him with her big green eyes and dark-bronze hair tied back in a ponytail.

'I just noticed you don't wear makeup. I like it.'

'Why so nice all of a sudden? Are you hitting on me?'

'Can I give you a compliment without you making a scene out of it?' he smiled, watching her cheeks flame.

'Maybe you can,' She smiled back and winked. 'now keep your eyes on the road unless you want to-- OH GOD HARRY! She flung up her hands defensively.

Harry tried to drive aside but the truck was too fast. It hit them at full speed. Their car spun out, hit another two cars and dropped into the river.

Kristen opened her eyes. The room was full of unpacked boxes lying on the floor. She looked at them and went straight to the kitchen. The phone beeped and she picked it up.

On the screen was an alert 'You have one voice message'. She dialed the number.

'I...'she briefly heard a female voice but buzzing static was breaking up the message.

Silence. She looked at her phone again.

'Okay...that was weird.' She lit up a cigarette, wondering who it was.

The phone rang. A chill ran down her spine. She answered the phone without looking.

'Who are you?'her voice quavered. 'Was that you on the message?'

'Kris? Are you okay? You sound weird. It's me, Adam.'

'Oh, Adam...right...,' she tried to get herself together 'What do you want?'

'Harsh,'he said, laughing. 'I'm in town. Are you free right now?'

'I might be.'

'So are you?'

'What do you wanna do? Bowling again?' she flicked her ash onto the floor.

'I'm never tired of bowling, but if you want to be fussy about it let's go somewhere else. Cafe Moonlight?'

'Does that place even exist anymore? I forgot about it.'

'Last time I checked it was there. Meet you there in an hour. See you babes.' He hung up.

She checked the time. It was almost 6pm. She threw off her robe and went to change her clothes with the burnt-to-the-filter cigarette still in her mouth. She washed the tip in the sink, threw it in the trash and tried to shake off her nerves. But as she was putting her makeup on, she couldn't stop thinking about the message.

The voice sounded so familiar, she thought as she brushed her hair, and looked at the phone lying on the table.

It was a rush hour and the pavement was as crowded as the street. People passed her seeming not to care whether they bumped her or not. She felt someone push her. Her bag fell on the concrete. She grabbed it before it was stepped on and spun around to see who had pushed her.

She saw a girl rushing to the crosswalk. Kristen ran after her and managed to grab her shoulder but the girl twisted away and sprinted across the street as the lights changed. She was the same height and had the same short dark-bronze hair as Kristen. She shrugged off her hand like it was a bug and crossed the road. Kristen stared at her walking away for a little longer. The girl turned around at the corner. Kristen saw herself on that corner. The shock hit her and her muscles tensed. She couldn't move. The girl was nowhere to be seen. As if she had evaporated. The colour drained from Kristen's face. She crossed the road to check the spot where she'd last seen the girl. She had the face of the girl, herself, vivid in her mind as if she was in front of her again. Those same big green eyes, long nose and full lips.

'She was so strong' she said to herself and a man passing by turned to flick a glance at her.

The Moonlight Cafe was right in front of her but she couldn't see Adam anywhere. She went inside. Some people were gathered near the stage.

'Excuse me, what's happening tonight?' she asked the boy cleaning up the tables

'Stand-ups. Some famous performers are coming too. Lot's of fun.' he said with a big smile on his face

'Right. Fun.' she said with no sign of interest and moved to the counter to buy some coffee.

She took an oat milk cappuccino and sat at a corner table the farthest from the stage. She crossed her legs and lit up a cigarette. There were more people coming in but no sign of Adam. She started to watch the whole room. She took a drag on her cigarette and flicked the ash on the floor. The lights dimmed. Minutes passed, she lit another cigarette. She took her time, sipping the cappuccino and peeking at the doors occasionally. The cafe was already full. People trying to move towards their seats were creating havoc. The stand-ups were just about to start. Kristen sighed, took the last sip of her coffee and got up. She started heading towards the exit. At the door, she reached for her phone and dialed Adam. No signal.

'As always you are not picking up that damn phone, you idiot. Thanks for ditching me tonight.' she said after the beep.

She sighed again and went out into the street. She decided to walk even though it was drizzling outside.

She was lying down on the bed with the cigarette in one hand and a drink in another. The clock struck noon. She took a long puff and looked at the window. Her eyes were wandering across the whole bedroom. She was staring at one point for a moment and then she was moving to another. The phone rang. It was Adam.

'Finaaallly' she thought.

'Bethany? I've heard your message . Why were you so upset? I didn't ditch you last night.'

'How did you call me? So now you are not only forgetting about your friends but also mixing their names. Well done Adam'

'I called you Bethany because you asked me to. Yesterday, remember? What was that message anyways?'

'Stop messing with me Adam. Can't you just apologise and stop finding excuses like always?'

'Okay I will. I apologise. Are you satisfied? Are you done with your little play?'

'I'm not playing. I was waiting for you at the cafe yesterday. I had a really shitty day and I wanted my old pal to be there for me, but you weren't.'

'You seemed okay yesterday. You were on your way to the cafe. That's when I saw you. Are you okay Kris?'

She gasped.

'What was she like? The other me?'

'Do you believe me now?'

'Tell me.'

'Yesterday you told me you never liked the name Kristen....'

'My mom gave me that name. You know my mother. The dominant b...woman that she is.'

' You insisted I call you Beth from now on. I was surprised with that change for a moment,' she heard him take a drag on a cigarette 'and you looked thinner too.' he laughed.

'What else?'

'You said you don't have that much time because you had to run some errands. You told me you will make it up to me.'

'I don't understand it. I was at the cafe. I took the same coffee I always have, sat at the same spot. You should've recognised she wasn't me.'

' Don't be so pissed off. How could I know.'

' I don't know. You are my best friend, aren't you?'

' You are being silly now. That girl looked like you. It was you. Anyways, I need to go back to work now. Would be good for you to do the same Kris, no more games.'

' I am trying to...'

' Try better. You can't live like that. Someday you won't have money for your cigs, what will you do then?'

' Thanks big brother.' She sighed 'I will keep this in mind. You need to go now. Bye.'

' Take ca..'

She hung up and threw the phone on the other side of the bed. She reached for the bottle of wine at the table and poured herself some more. She had a few sips and dozed off with the glass in her hand.

The dark water twirled like ballet dancers in an opera. She found herself deep down there. She was looking for something. She saw a car with no one inside. She swam closer to it searching for some clues. She felt something almost next to the car. She saw a hand and a golden ring. She tried to swim closer. She reached out her hand. The water started swirling faster and faster. She lost sight of the hand and the ring. She woke up and saw white walls. She looked around. It was a hospital. She couldn't feel anything. She heard someone whispering at the door. She noticed someone had brought her flowers. The name on the card was Beth. Beth Swan.

The phone call woke her up. The glass she was holding in her hand crashed to the floor. She looked at the screen. It was her mom.

Awesome. This cannot be good, she thought.

She was still a little dizzy and trying to hold onto last night's dream. She ignored the call. A message popped up 'Come visit me tomorrow. Love you, Mom'. She rolled her eyes.

'I came as you asked me to. Where is Pa?'

A woman in her mid-sixties approached her and tried to hug her. Kristen stepped back.

'He is away.' the woman said with a sad look on her face

'Another business trip? Always busy as a bee. Maybe that is why he was always so disappointed in me...because I'm not like him'

'Stop saying such things. Now come have dinner with me. I have made you your favourite strawberry milkshake.' the woman said with a smile.

Wrinkles on her face looked like the very thin lines of a map.

'I don't like strawberries. Never did. Especially milkshakes.'

'You always liked it, you had one the last time you were here, I will make you something else then.'

'Don't bother. Why did you want me here? I don't remember us ever being chatty.'

Mom looked at her and frowned for a moment.

'Come to the living room and we'll talk. I think it's time.'

It was already late. She dialed Adam. She waited a few beeps.

'Hello you.' she heard his voice over the phone

'Come over.'

She hung up. She was standing next to one of the boxes in her apartment. Her large green eyes turned to the box with unease. When she opened it she flinched. She saw photos of her and a man. A tall man with ginger hair. They were both smiling. In one of the photos she could see her mom in the background. She took her phone to find that voice message again.

' I... ' she could briefly heard the female voice but the buzz...

Silence. She played it over and over again. She blanched.

Someone knocked on the door.

'It's open.' she shouted

It was Adam.

'Is someone dead?' he said

'I remember.'

'What are you talking about?

'I...'

'Are you...'

'I...Harry is dead.'

'Who is Harry? You've never mentioned him.'

'My mom told me what happened. The accident. We were coming to a family gathering. I fell out with my parents over the phone. I...'

'Maybe sit here...' he pointed the sofa

'Can you help me open those boxes?'

'What happened next? What were you saying?'

'I started some silly fight. At least he thought so.' she continued

'Who was he to you?'

'He was my husband. Can you open that one first?' she pointed the box with the caption 'Harry'

He picked up a knife lying next to the box and cut a hole in it.

'I think Kris doesn't know Harry dead.'

'Who are you?'
'I...My name is Beth. Beth Swan.'

THE END

HILLS OF SPRING, TEL AVIV
BY
ANDREI KURBYKO

It was the shortest day of the year when I finally dared to go to the airport. Gray miserable haze, for a moment, became a blanket of mist but as we gained some altitude the Sun finally touched my cheek. I realized that we haven't engaged for months. The town, somewhere below, was completely hidden by the clouds so I was finally invisible to it. It was a pleasant feeling. I was afraid it would always be like that.

Three hours later I was standing on the doorsteps of the White City. It smelled like jasmine and garbage and it was slowly waking up from the Sabbath. I looked up at the sky and the stars could see me clearly from their dark December den.

Naor was kind enough to let me occupy one of his empty rooms. It was on the last floor of one of those houses whose destiny is ambiguous and untold. It could have been built eighty years ago or maybe just eight, but houses are worthless without their tenants.

Naor's flat did not change at all, neither did he. A poster of America directing its people to the new frontier on his wall was more faded and its paper was slightly wavy after days of storms. Heaps of Penguin books and free journals were bigger, dried branches of cotton were not. Time had a different style of the ruling here. Days started in the evening, weeks started on Sundays, seasons were blurry, a holiday mess with golden lights and decorated trees did not exist. The year was not going to end with boisterous parties and fireworks in ten days. Most importantly, time here was kinder.

The latest news of the flat was a mouse who, allegedly, came from nowhere and found a new home in the veranda, invisibly scratching under numerous cupboards, the carcasses of someone's paintings and stands with empty flowerpots. Naor speculated it was not alone. A newly bought cage-trap was placed, unmistakably clumsily, under a green ornate sofa, with a slowly rotting mango inside. I knew everything about mice, I understood them. One would never leave its sheltered place, especially without having something behind its back. Mice run only along walls. They stay in the dimness. I moved the cage under a table, next to the window. The Hanukkah menorah on the table was made of blue-water glass, so the candles would levitate, almost weightless, with lights glaring through the the glass and spreading all over the room. They were nicely prepared and placed right next to the menorah. The feast was starting tomorrow. The menorah was the only suggestion of this, different, holiday in the house, if not mentioning some donuts in the fridge. In fact, there was no holiday as I know it, with rich decorations, mild fruitful smells and days of expectations. Nothing could dare to change the ordinary routine, way of life calculated to be eased, soothing and not over pressing. Every day was a holiday, and the city, seen from the window of Naor's flat, was ready for it, replying with the usual sounds of sirens, shadows of party music, cries of children, swishings of Egyptian bats in the night and a light zephyr blowing from the sea.

Maoz tzur y'shuati
l'cha naeh l'shabeach
Tikon beit t'filati
v'sham todah n'zabeach.

Over time, I began to like returning somewhere much more than finding new places. In the city of my childhood, the first thing I do is walk down a familiar street. I'm no longer worried when I wander the slope where I broke my left knee as a kid. After changing countries, it became a ritual, played every few years, each time getting a feeling of complete satisfaction that never lasts long. I love the street I lived on as a student and my heart stops every time I walk past a cafe where I had my first date. I never go to bed early, but this time I decided to wrap up in a blanket waiting for tomorrow. Returning was my only plan.

Early morning, I was on the crowded boulevard. The orange fruit kiosk was about to open, its owner was running around, trying to clean fallen leaves and pour some water in a big shiny doggie drinker. Joggers were guessing that I am a stranger, I was thinking the same. A young mother was holding her child, who just fell a moment ago. She smiled at me and her slightly tired eyes were kind. My trench coat was fluttering, trying to catch the end of a burning cigarette. I did not care. An elderly couple just went out of the house and got stuck at the crossroad. They seemed to have just come down from the age of tiaras and butlers which is no longer here. She, with every detail and every gesture, looked like a princess, he matched her perfectly. How could she find herself here, among palm trees and shuks, and feel in place? She happened to leave her hat at home, an unacceptable mistake for the age. A mistake worth frustration, not another walk on the steep tiled staircase. He was trying to comfort the princess by smoothing her silver hair, shattered in the wind. She was trying to pretend that nothing has happened. They continued, holding hands. I went down the street to the sea.

L'eit tachin matbeach
mitzar hamnabeach
Az egmor b'shir mizmor
chanukat hamizbeach

When the time came, the first candle of eight was lightened. Its warmth was spreading around the room and the sulfur smell of matches was still in the air. Fire, weak and wavy at the beginning, was gaining its strengths, forming a calm gentle pillar of flame. Naor whispered a blessing, running his finger through the old pages of his pocketbook, a thing of habit as he knew the text from the childhood. The candle flame was gently moving in tune with the air, and there was nothing more stable and firm in the world that that flame. I hardly understood something from his mutter but refused to admit. The oldest spoken language in the world remembered centuries of such whispers. My Refuge, my Rock of Salvation! Then we will celebrate with song and psalm the altar's dedication. The Age would have no time to be present in the room with us, but as my friend started to sing a holiday psalm I felt that time was on our side. Seven more nights I spent sitting on a deckchair, clutching my knees and watching the mystery without contributing.

The White City transforms in the evening and the first stars bring light to its different nature. No matter where we would go, there was no salvation from the unseen eyes of street cats. They were everywhere, sneaking in shadows or staring at us from the height of brick walls. They were watching me but with no trust, disappearing as I approached. Endless car parks were interchanging with piles of old bikes and scooters, unwanted furniture or potentially wanted shelves full of books. I found a shiny gilded ring, left on the edge of a fountain. We ended up at a pub, as it started to rain. December storms are always sudden but never last for a while.

We were good friends because, after knowing each other for years, we were never disappointed. Our months were spent in swapping books, arguing 'what is true beauty' and debating current events. A man needs to be heard and hear in response, this is the power of such a relationship. We were different like valleys and forests, it was wonderful. We did not talk much that evening and I was happy to be back. Naor was tired and never could call himself a going-out person. His days, unlike mine, were about calmness, and I was never jealous. This contrast only gave me extra strength to run without looking back, afraid of being late for something I didn't even know I had. The most troublesome part of the journey is always to reach the top of the hill. It was always so crucial for me since only the silhouette on the top could be seen by the others. Hard to remember that to be in plain sight is to be vulnerable. Naor only smiled back.

I never smoked much like that night. The bitter taste of tobacco was mixed with the tartness of ale and the freshness of air. My friend was probably reading at home, the bar was taking last orders. The noisy bartender was speaking French. Tipsy companies were passing my window, night buses stopped at the traffic light of the square. The lights were reflected from the sidewalk and the empty multicolored chairs were left standing under cypresses. Somewhere far away was the music. The last customers brought a cart of sweets, they weren't here for the beer. Five or six guys in wide hats and black jackets, religious, came to share the holiday with everyone. There was a chandelier on the bar, the music moved into space, the dance followed the song.

Az egmor b'shir mizmor
chanukat hamizbeach

The sleepy houses around the square reflected these sounds as I walked outside. A waste truck with bright yellow wig-wags passed by me. It was a couple of blocks away from the house, I decided to run to the end. Now, only noisy footsteps disturbed the quiet of the night. I ran, under fruit trees, past sleepy cats, through cafes with cluttered tables, galleries with dripping air conditioners, past closed stalls of old junkmen, under neon signs of pharmacies and exchangers, kiosks selling lottery tickets and cigarettes, night shops owned by Arabs, through empty bus stops and memorial parks, not paying attention to all the languid ticking of traffic lights. We ran through the measured sleep of some city dwellers and in the exhausted fatigue of all tourists, overtaking sad taxi drivers and returning night shifters, past all turns to calm alleys and middles of wide green boulevards, past the lonely lights on a top of some houses and candle reflections in windows. Two teenagers with a scooter, winding in circles, singing hava nagila. I warbled in reply.

I could not tell the day when Naor woke me up. The Sun was going to rise in an hour. He said not a word, waving and letting me follow straight to the next room. There were all eight candles, it was my last day.

Underneath, finally trapped, was a small little mouse terrified even more than us two, in the corner. We decided to go to the park, right next to the house, where two rivers join each other just to flow to the sea. Two figures in long coats disturbed the calm of the place, one of them held a small cage in hands. Passing through long alleys and deserted grounds, they chose a bench by a pier, overlooking the river and the thickets of high grass. Above their heads, in the morning haze, a plane flew slowly, flashing sidelights. It retreated towards the horizon. When the mouse saw the door open, it froze for a moment, as if thinking, and then hid in the grass. Two figures stayed on the bench looking at the gray and blue morning. It was not until dozens of minutes later that they noticed a slight sway in the green, as if something was still there. Shyly and carefully walking along the shore, without waking up sleepy ducks, the park inhabitant appeared next to the water's edge. The jackal had no fear of people. Stopping and breathing in the morning air. He stared at two silhouettes in coats, moving his ears in different ways. They locked eyes on each other in silence. Then another ran up, rolling in the sand and lifting the splashes, then they played lightly biting each other. A little farther away, more scared, too small to leave their hiding place, two jackal puppies were seen.

I knew that he wanted to travel like me. But I wanted to stop all returnings, keeping all as it was. The plane was not delayed, gates closed on time, and a small noisy bus brought me straight to the liner. On the way, we passed the skeleton of an enormous Boeing, which was slowly falling apart. Not white anymore, with no engines and faded liveries, it was napping while waiting for merciful time to digest it.

Three hours from then I was going to disappear in mists, as they were ready to take me back.

THE END

SO CLOSE
BY
SARAH WILHELM

I was nothing but pure liquid black evil. They changed me. Those girls, they changed me and now I sat here looking at myself staring at nothing. I was nothing. The focus I had on myself was miraculous as my insides scratched at me viciously trying to get out. I knew all their secrets. I could rat them out and let their billions of dollars flood the streets, but they knew mine and if they told them, my life would be over.

It's funny how manipulation happens. I wonder if people even realize if it is really happening to them? I thought I was smart, maybe even smarter than average. What you find out is, it's never the case. There is always someone smarter, prettier, better than you in every way possible. The worst part? Life will always smack you right in the face with better people, especially when you actually start showing you mean something to the world.

I could not stop looking at myself. It was as if every mirror knew where I was, and the gravitational pull was undeniable. I could hear the voices in my head lightly whispering that someone else was more beautiful, more intelligent, more unique. It was like I became the person that I dreaded to be my whole life. I could instantly feel bad about myself and I read that to become 'more beautiful' you must look at others you admire. Copy their look.

My thoughts immediately turned to social media. The land of the fake. Fake happiness, fake beauty. If you did not face tune yourself, were you even going to get a like? Beauty was my obsession. It was the perceptions of others that I was obsessed over. I could watch people look at a beautiful person and treat them entirely better than an average looking person. The nature of beauty became my obsession. Spending hours searching every social media site out there to study the beauty of others was my specialty. Why couldn't I find such beauty in myself?

My head felt the pressure of life pulsating, repetitively. I paced back and forth, stopping at the mirror to look at myself and then continuing again to pace. This repeated for hours. After severely analyzing myself, I came to a conclusion about what was wrong with me. My face was too fat. My legs and arms jiggled with every movement I made. I could definitely create another human out of my stomach and the hair on my head was just fragile pieces of hay. Everything was wrong. Everything looked nothing like the pictures online.

'Look at you, you're nothing. Those girls from your class, they are way better than you. They have money, cars, designer this and that. And what do you have? You have fat all around you. That's it. Nobody likes you. Not even you. You dumb bit-' Was I really prepared to say that about myself?

Holding that mirror with my two hands, I stared straight into my eyes, 'You're not a dumb bitch.'

I was trembling to say those words out loud. Tears fell down my face ruining my makeup. I wanted to give myself a hug. I needed one, for just once in my life I really needed a fucking hug.

I sat down in my tub with a blue metallic journal of mine, clicked my pen and started calculating. I started by putting my two hands around my upper thighs to see how much distance there was left between my fingertips. 'So close' I thought. If I could just lose 10 pounds to be the same weight as I was in high school. And if I could burn 500 calories a day at the gym and eat 1,200 calories a day, I could be at my goal weight in two months.

My fingertips would eventually lead me to search engines. I would half-consciously and subconsciously type in the names of celebrities who have the same weight and height as me. It was endless. I would then search for more ridiculous things such as 'how to scientifically become more beautiful.' Which would lead me to 'how to contour your face to look like someone else.' The pain I was feeling was not pain as I had known pain before, it had a different quality. Before, it was me feeling I didn't deserve to feel beautiful but now it was feeling I had to be the most beautiful of all. My mind was racing, giving me a high that was uncontrollable. It wasn't normal to feel such things, but what was normal anymore?

Poland against the all-American girl. Didn't seem so hard to start a whole new life in an entirely different country when you are 20 years old, or at least that was my thought process. I was young, outgoing, full of life and nothing could stop me. The only fear I had was not accomplishing the dreams that sat deep inside that pure heart of mine. I guess you could definitely say that going to Europe was a dream I had. Maybe not Poland particularly but it didn't matter because I was finally able to move across the world to go to college, but also be with the man I loved.

Many said I was naïve, others said ambitious but either way people were nothing but surprised when I told them I was moving to Warsaw, Poland. When they say that love really can make you do anything, that was surely the fucking truth. So, here I was, Miss. All-American, with my three suitcases traveling across the world to be with someone who I thought truly cared about me.

When I arrived, everything was beautiful. I literally felt the energy of life for the first time. The excitement was unbearable, and I could finally see why people said that life is beyond where you stay. Everything about me became different. I walked different, talked different, fuck I even glowed different. It wasn't just me who noticed me, everyone did. People started coming up to me asking where I was from, and was surprised that I came all the way from America. I was unique here and I loved it. My positivity was contagious and I never wanted it to stop.

A week after arriving and moving into my first apartment with my boyfriend, I had to start college. Talk about a whole bunch of new things at once, but I didn't care. My happiness took over any fear. I put on a pair of jeans, a cute pink shirt and a white pair of Vans. My backpack was trendy yet casual and I felt as if I was ready to start my journey towards International Business Management. This is where I was meant to be, I just knew it.

As I walked into the school's outside entrance, my mouth almost dropped and hit the floor. These people were nothing like what I had ever seen in my life. They were the most beautiful people I had ever laid my eyes on. They glistened as if they were born from diamonds. The men looked like they came right off the runway of Italy. Hair perfectly positioned, clothes ironed, their shoes matched their designer belts. They were nothing but handsome.

The women, I swear were on a whole other level of life. They wore dresses, skirts, jumpsuits, heels, furs, designer everything, the list could go on and let's just say, no one had a backpack. Their hair was perfectly shiny, and long. Did they even wear makeup because everyone's skin was gorgeous.

I found a bathroom as soon as possible to look at my kindergarten outfit. Wow, I thought. I have to step it up. I walked out, embarrassed about my outfit, but slowly walked towards my class room N129. I sat nervously waiting for a teacher like person to come open the door to let me in. Across from me was a beautiful woman. Long blonde hair, perfectly applied makeup with a unique deep black winged eyeliner that framed her face perfectly. She wore an outfit similar to mine which made me instantly feel better. She smiled at me, and I smiled back. Our teacher came seconds after, and I was relieved to get out of this hallway full of models.

Class started shortly as the teacher introduced herself. The class was called, how to start a business 101. Ten minutes went by and she asked us to stand up and get into groups. I decided to sit next to the girl who smiled at me.

'Hi, I'm Jane, would you like to be partners?'

'I would love to.' Her eyes lit up.

'Sweet, what's your name?'

'Lea, nice to meet you.'

'Nice to meet you too. Are you from Poland?'

'Yes, but I was born in California then moved here when I was three. Where are you from?'

'Wisconsin.' She smiled.

'Figured you were from the States. We should hang out sometime, you seem cool.'

'Yeah, that would be awesome, I don't-' The teacher cut me off.

'Alright everyone we are going to get started, please take your seats.'

I looked at her and nodded. She nodded back, settling a nonverbal agreement that we would talk about later. As I was listening to what the task was, I dropped my pen on the floor. When I went to pick it up, I saw Lea's purse.

It was a black leather purse and in gold print were the words 'Prada.'

THE END

WRITING ADVICE
BY
BULENT AKMAN

My approach is trial-and-error combined with some deductive tinkering.

If something works, do more of it, if it doesn't, do less of it. Your world, your rules. Experiment. Take notes. Invent your own rules.

Kurt Vonnegut had two. They are enough.

First, In every scene, characters must want something even if it's only a glass of water. Second, every story can be plotted on an axis of good and bad fortune through time.

I have 10 rules.

1. Start with a character or a situation in a place because everything happens somewhere.

2. Start at the beginning, middle or end and write out from there.

3. Write every day. No exceptions. Have a beginning, middle and end. Regardless of quality.

4. We come to stories to feel first and think second. Thinking is good but isn't impactful without emotion.

5. Every scene must have conflict. Conflict is the heart of drama, drama is the heart of fiction.

6. Description slows down the story. Action and dialogue speeds it up.

7. Only describe details that are unusual, otherwise you're getting in the way of your audience.

8. Action and dialogue are more important than description.

9. Characters to be interesting need only be clearly written and in trouble.

10. Ideas fall like cosmic radiation on everyone equally so carry a

notebook. Be ready to catch them.

Writers are the same as everybody, they just take notes. William S. Burroughs said that but he also shot his wife in the forehead during a party stunt that went wrong. All of which goes to show that writing won't save you if that's what you're hoping. The only person who can do that is you. Towards that end, write what you really want to write. Be fearless. Come in. The water's fine. This early in the season there are few monsters.

I have two stories for aspiring writers but they are to all artists in general. I heard them long ago and this is how I remember them.

The maestro visited a small town for a concert, a young violinist persuaded the maestro to hear their audition. The aspiring musician asked the maestro afterwards if they were good enough to go to the city and audition for the symphony. The maestro said 'No, you haven't got what it takes.'

Many years later, the maestro visited the town again. After the concert someone approached the maestro. “You may not remember me but I auditioned for you years ago. I am very happy I took your advice. I live in a lovely home with my wonderful spouse and beautiful children but tell me, did I really not have any talent at all?”

The maestro said “You had talent but I tell everyone who asks that they haven't got what it takes, because if my telling you is enough to stop you than you really don't have what it takes.”

Mozart was asked at what age someone should attempt their first symphony and he replied they should try something simpler like an arrangement for a string quartet and even that should not be attempted before spending several years in intense study and formal schooling. The person was surprised by the answer and said “but you wrote your first symphony when you were a child!”

“Yes,” replied Mozart, “but I didn't ask permission.”

So begin before you are ready. Submit and be rejected. If you wait until you are ready you will never begin, neither will you ever be ready.

So go. Write. Fail. Write. Fail again. Fail better. Write on.

Warsaw, Friday September 24, 2021

Permissions

ABOUT THIS ANTHOLOGY

Contemporary Stories of Otherness is the second volume in a series of collected student creative fiction.

We, the editors, believe that affording our students the opportunity to see their work in print is an essential component of developing creative writing skills.

Special Thanks to CreateSpace which has democratized the means of publishing for the benefit of all. To find out more, visit: https://www.createspace.com/ and start your book project today. Begin before you are ready! If you wait until you are ready you will find someone is already there.

www.ingramcontent.com/pod-product-compliance
Lightning Source LLC
LaVergne TN
LVHW010510160826
845677LV00012B/2766

* 9 7 9 8 4 8 1 6 0 7 2 1 4 *